THE LAST CLIMB

A Missoula Flood Short Story

Shannon Skaer

CONTENTS

preface

At the close of the Ice Age, the Pacific Northwest was hit by a catastrophe we call the Missoula Flood. Moving faster than 60mph and over 800 ft deep in places, the flood scoured more than 50 cubic miles of matter from Washington State, a quarter of which was deposited in the Willamette Valley, Oregon, and adjacent areas. The rest washed out to sea. We don't know if there were people in the area at the time, but if there were, this is what they might have seen.

Any resemblance between the customs and persons in this story and those of any extant tribe or nation is purely coincidental.

THE LAST CLIMB

The earth began to vibrate as we neared the village. Bleached grass rustled, flattened against the sloping valley walls by last winter's snows. The surface of the wide brown river sparkled in the afternoon sunlight with strange little ripples. The movement went on and on, as gentle, as deadly, as the panic that rose in my chest.

Three months ago, I'd have been curious, just a boy ready for adventure. Then Father died and I became Chief. Now whatever danger lay in the waking earth and shivering grass was mine to face. Behind me, my little brother Cusi chattered on, his words and the ripple of the river nearly masking a sound so soft that my ears could not tell me when it began, or where it came from. A roar, a hum, like a beehive—only deeper and nearer.

"We need a better stick," Cusi said. "This one cuts into my shoulder. I told you we needed a different one."

I glanced back, but the deer carcass suspended on a pole between us blocked his face. All I could see were two hooves tied with a strip of fresh rawhide. "Do you hear that noise?" I asked.

"You should have cut the deer in pieces back where we killed it. Then it wouldn't be so heavy. Wait—wait, stop. I need to switch shoulders."

I stood, staring at a nodding spike of spring wildflowers. Here, behind the shelter of a rocky outcropping that jutted into the narrow valley, the air was still. Some other force touched the purple blossoms and set them trembling. I turned my head from side to side, trying to catch the source of the sound echoing across the river and back from the hills on the other side. Behind us? From the mountains to the left? "Cusi..."

"I know why you didn't cut it in pieces," Cusi said. "You wanted the whole tribe to see that the new chief could. . . What's wrong? What's that sound? Is it following us?"

I didn't blame him for the fear in his voice. The dancing earth made my heart race, but the noise. . . the noise left me looking behind each boulder for shelter, staring into each patch of brambles, straining my eyes like a rabbit in a snare. What would Father do? *Master your fear, use your eyes, make a plan.* That's what he taught me. My eyes and ears told me something unnatural was happening. My plan?

I dropped my gaze. "I don't know. Let's go." Whatever this danger was, my place was with my people. I moved forward. The branch on my shoulder jerked as Cusi started after me a moment too late.

"Is it an earthquake?" Cusi panted, "Tupak, is it an earthquake?"

Master your fear.

We rounded the bend in the river and our village lay before us: longhouses scattered beside a gleaming brook, which ran down the slope into the river under a clear, windswept sky. The valley widened here, and beyond the lone pine, the fields lay green with new spring growth. Could I have imagined it? There in the open, it was hard to see if the earth still moved, but the noise was clearer, murmuring back from the valley walls.

Use your eyes.

Cries came from the longhouses as women called their children close. Dicali, the priest—the old vulture—stood by the path that ran along the river bank. As we passed, his sharp eyes darted our way and he twitched his heavy necklace straight. Should I speak to him? He might expect it. After all, I was Chief, but what would I say?

Make a plan.

I put my head down and moved on.

"Slow down," Cusi said. "Tupak, it must be an earthquake."

We reached our house and dropped the weight from our shoulders. It was unfair. How could I make a plan to protect people from something so unnatural?

"Children of the River," Dicali marched to the foot of the pine tree. "Children of the River, gather to me!" Warriors approached him, weapons clutched tight, eyes darting between the earth and the branches of the tree waving overhead. Real warriors. Men who had hunted and fought for more summers than I'd been alive.

Here was the first true test of my leadership, and Dicali had taken my place. No one looked to me, and for a moment I was glad of it. Maybe Dicali had a plan.

I knelt and touched the ground. The earth pulsed through my hands, up my arms, into my body. Tiny grains of dirt hopped and skittered. The dry taste of dust filled my mouth as it rose from the hard-packed soil. I stood, recoiling from the living thing under my feet. The blood drained from my head, leaving my ears ringing.

Cusi moved away, open-mouthed, towards the old priest.

"The Watchers are angry," Dicali screamed above the rising clamor. "We must read the omens!"

"Chief," said a voice by my side. It was Old Mother, the stranger among us, a midwife come to deliver Meernan's child. Old Mother was a tiny, crooked woman, who stood like she owned the village. Age lined her face, but her eyes were bright and worried. "Chief, something evil comes. I've felt this before, I know this sound. I once lived far from here on a great plain. There lived herds so numerous that it took a day for them to pass. And when they approached, the earth felt like it does now—almost. Something is coming."

"This is no earthquake of the world," Dicali cried. "We are cursed! The Earth-God shakes his head in anger!"

I fixed my eyes on Old Mother. "What is coming?" The movement could be anything, and it was my valley, the familiar mountains I'd known from childhood, that shook. But the sound came from somewhere else. Some*thing* else.

"I don't know." She shivered. "We should move to higher ground, climb the mountain. It is the only way to safety."

"Safety from what? We are warriors. We do not run without cause." And yet it was a plan, even if it made no sense.

Her eyes dropped. She had no answer.

"Tupak," Dicali called to me, "Bring the animal!"

Would my father have told someone else to lift the carcass, sling it across his back? Another day I would have time to answer that question, but not today, not with a yellow cloud of pollen shaking down from the pine tree, twisting away into nothingness on a cold east wind.

Old Mother laid her hand on my arm. "We must climb the mountain. A monster comes!"

I shook off her hand and walked toward Dicali, trying to imitate Father's confident stride.

Dicali's hands slipped in the blood, digging through the animal's entrails for omens, and his lips formed soundless pleas. He wiped the sweat away with the back of his hand and left a red smear behind, bright against the gray pallor of his face. "There is no heart," he muttered. "No heart."

The people crowded around the priest and carcass.

"Mercy, mercy!" Dicali babbled. "Earth, hear your children, or we are lost!" He took his knife and dragged it across his cheeks until the blood ran, first one side, then the other, eyes rolling from one man to the next. "We must offer a sacrifice, a great sacrifice."

Behind him stood Old Mother, arms crossed on her meager chest, watching me. Everyone jerked as a dead branch shook loose from the nearby tree, everyone but her. She had mastered her fear. The old priest was fear itself, and his fear infected my people. Every creature has a heart.

I stepped forward, plunged my hand into the fresh carcass jiggling on the stained dirt, cut out the heart, and threw it at Dicali's feet. "Here it is. We will climb the mountain and see what we can find."

Dicali stared at the heart, took a stumbling step backward and looked at me for the first time.

"Child, what do you know of the gods? How dare you lay your hand to the omens? Do you want to bring more evil upon us?"

I knew little of the gods, but the priest was no leader for my people, and the roar was growing louder, carried on the wind. "You missed the heart. I found it—"

"You know nothing." He stepped toward me until his foul breath warmed my face. "How many summers have you seen, sixteen?"

I stood straighter. "Eighteen. Enough to find a heart when I look for one. What else are you missing, Dicali?" The words sounded brave enough.

Another branch fell with a crack, a larger one.

"Madmen!" Dicali shrieked, starting back. "How long will you stand talking? Until the Earth-God vomits fire? We must make the great sacrifice!"

I knew of what he spoke. A human sacrifice had not been made since before my father's time. And if he made that sacrifice once, he could make it again, and again. Power would be his. "No," I said, in a voice I barely recognized. "This could be only a fire-mountain. We will climb and see."

"No time!" Dicali waved a fist in my direction. "No time. We must sacrifice."

"Who is the chieftain here, Dicali? Stay and read omens if you choose, but we will climb the mountain." I turned and walked away, not daring to look back. Would they follow? Should I force Dicali to come?

Cusi joined me. "Why are we going up the mountain? Are you certain about this?"

Just what I needed, my little brother second-guessing my decision. "Are they following?" I whispered through clenched teeth.

"What?"

"*Are they following?*" I'd look a fool if I climbed the mountain alone.

He glanced back. "Yes, some are."

Voices rose behind me. I should have made Dicali follow me. What was I thinking, leaving him to infect the others with his mindless fear? I could still turn around and seize him, drag him up the mountain—but to turn would look weak. I could not appear weak.

The climb was long and steep. The wind tugged at us, growing stronger and colder with every step. When we were far enough away, I snuck glances at the village. Who would go, who would stay? Too many stayed. Even then, I could have turned. I could have made them follow, but I did not.

I did not.

When we climbed high enough to see past the walls of the narrow river valley, all was peaceful. Far to the northeast lay the great king-peak of Takeema, the fountain of milk-white waters, crowned with ice, slumbering in the sunlight. Next came Kill-Kay-tac, and southward, beyond the river, the peak of Wyeest. Closer still was the summit of Louwyth, sending a gentle plume of ash rising lazily in the air. A fire-mountain, then, but not one that could cause this shaking. Later, perhaps tonight, ash might fall and fire leap from the mountaintop. Not yet.

The quivering had grown more violent, or did it only seem so, from that height?

No, stronger.

And the noise, no longer a murmur but an angry roar, the echoes rolling back from the mountains.

Birds flew screaming into the air. Animals sprang out of the brush and dashed crazily from one hiding spot to another. A warrior passed me, falling and rising again, scrambling on all fours. I turned, scanning the valley below.

A cloud, a dark mist, raced from the east, where a little hill, three times the height of a man, hid the winding river. A strange little cloud, rolling, moving faster than a man can run.

And then the hill was gone, vanished, and in its place a dark wall, moving at tremendous speed.

I rubbed my eyes and blinked, looked again.

What was this new terror? A hole, rent in the fabric of the world, gaping and growing bigger, swallowing all in darkness?

It was a wave, choked with mud and debris, carving through the solid rock as effortlessly as if it were a child's sand-hill. It raced toward the village with terrible swiftness and its roar shook the earth.

I gasped for air that would not come. My people shrieked in terror, calling on the gods to save them or clinging to one another. Many were strung out between the village and the mountaintop. My people, my tribe, in the path of that monster. Below me struggled a warrior carrying a child, clutching the hand of his pregnant wife. Two more little ones, a boy and girl, straggled behind.

I ran, sliding, leaping from rock to rock down towards the children. Before me the dark wave gobbled the vivid green of the sun-drenched valley. The village below disappeared in a single heartbeat, the fields and houses, the lone pine gone in the hungry torrent.

A bramble tore my leg and I tumbled, snatching at a sapling to slow my fall. I scraped to a stop, crouched on all fours.

The wave thundered away down the river's path, but the water in its wake only rose, higher and higher still. The wave had been the monster's head—now came the shoulders, shoving the very mountains apart as they swelled into a space too small for their crowding depths.

I stumbled to my feet and scrambled down the mountain toward the screaming children. With every stride I took, the water rose five.

It spread long dark hands, fingering the hillside, tearing the ground until it fell away in great chunks into the swirling mud.

It took Meernan. It took beautiful black-eyed Kaloua with her sister's child in her arms. Rintac and his family fell, one after another. The roar of water drowned their cries.

And still it rose. We were insects before it, crawling flies, scattering before the unstoppable torrent.

Quhata and his sons, halfway up the mountain, turned to look. The ground beneath them churned as it fell.

I reached the children and snatched them up. A blast of icy wind tossed me and we hit the ground, soaked with a sudden shock of spray. I swung the girl on my back and her arms wound tight around my neck. I loosed her grip with my free hand and caught a breath. The other child I clutched to my chest as I crawled upwards, grasping at clumps of grass.

The climb went on forever. Now stumbling, now crawling, with always the child's wail in my ear and the spray of freezing water soaking my legs. No time, only scraped hands and fear like blindness and the taste of mud.

Lifetimes later, the roar lessened.

I turned and sat in the dirt of that hillside, pulled the children onto my lap, and willed my chattering teeth to silence.

The sun set, as it has so many times before. The water flowed on, its surface black with mud and masses of dirt-stained ice.

I rocked the weeping children back and forth, back and forth, until their father crawled to claim them. I rolled on my side and clutched the quivering grass with both fists. Now I could cry, but no tears came.

I must have slept. I woke in darkness, blacker than any night of this earth, with Cusi's warm body huddled against mine and the earth still humming beneath us. The noise of the water had subsided into a constant low roar, and flakes, soft as dust, fell upon us all around. Ash. It softened all other sounds, and except for the occasional peal of thunder, the air was heavy and close. The stench of sulfur strangled my breath.

How many of my people had I lost? I should have made them come before it was too late—Father would have done so. Not me. I was afraid to look soft.

When the sun rose, it cast a faint glow upon ghosts with dazed eyes and faces gray with ash, huddled in a world unmade. I padded from one knot of survivors to another, counting. Old Mother cradled an orphaned child, with tear-streaks running down the smudge of ash on his little round face. She believed the water came from the draining of an upland ocean, like spring floods bursting through a beaver's dam. If she was right, the water would soon be gone, carrying with it the life we once knew.

Tolam, Puntic and his family. . . each person I found living was a gift, and each one missing added to my guilt. Only twenty-three remained, and before this, our tribe counted seventy-one. Seventy-two, with Meernan's babe.

That first morning I got them up and led them westward, along the tops of the new cliffs carved away by the torrent, but it was no use. Just below us, the monster surged on with the force and speed of a cataract. We all felt its presence, its grumble in the earth. It took the air from our lungs and the strength from our legs. Tolam's boy turned to stone when he saw the water, his body curled in a rigid knot, teeth shaking, and some of the other children did the same.

After that I chose a different path, far enough away to keep the water out of sight, but close enough not to lose my way. Only Old Mother walked by the cliffs, watching the farther bank for signs of the valley where her people lived, stumping along with her staff in hand and her eyes like a hawk's. Each day the water rushed on a little lower than the day before.

On the third day I led them south, searching for summer hunting grounds untouched by the wave, and tribes who could trade us seed so life could begin again. No one questioned my decision, not even the oldest warrior. They blessed me, even in their grief and shock. But I know what they would not understand, must not understand.

I could have saved more.

WHAT WAS THE MISSOULA FLOOD?

BY MICHAEL J. OARD, AUTHOR OF LIFE IN THE GREAT ICE AGE

The Lake Missoula flood was likely the largest super flood in the world.[12] When ice from the Ice Age slowly melted, it generated massive flooding. Melting glaciers filled the valleys of western Montana trapped behind an ice dam in northern Idaho that blocked the Clark Fork River. The ice dam was formed by a finger of the Cordilleran Ice Sheet in British Columbia and adjacent northern Washington, northern Idaho, and northwest Montana. Behind the dam, glacial Lake Missoula gradually rose until it reached 2,000 feet deep near the dam. By then it had a volume of about 500 cubic miles—around four times Lake Erie's volume and half Lake Michigan's volume. Suddenly, it burst and emptied in about two days.

The flood waters roared across northern Idaho into Washington and Oregon, cutting and shaping the land. They formed the Camas Prairie ripples, northwest of Missoula, Montana, and gravel ridges from 15 to 50 feet high. The water sped at about 60 mph carrying rocks and dirt through the constriction of Eddy Narrows. The Narrows, between Plains and Thompson Falls, Montana, are less than a mile wide and 10 miles long. The deluge was about 180 m deep when it covered the current location of Spokane, Washington. As it raced 80 mph and 1,000 feet deep it rushed through the Columbia Gorge between Washington and Oregon and spread to 400 feet deep west of the Columbia Gorge. The Native Americans would have felt the ground shaking and a loud roaring a half hour before the waters overwhelmed them. The flood eroded 50 cubic miles of soft Palouse silt and hard basalt from eastern Washington in about a week.

Before the flood entered the Columbia Gorge, it had to navigate a constriction at Wallula Gap, south of Pasco, Washington. This caused the water to back up and form a temporary lake 800 ft deep, called Lake Lewis. As the lake filled, the flood water backwashed up the tributaries to the Columbia River: the Snake, Walla Walla, and Yakima River Valleys. Since the water was filled with sediment, it deposited 40 alternating sand/silt layers over 100 feet deep in the Walla Walla River Valley when it slowed. Lake Lewis is believed to have drained in about a week.

The water's velocity greatly decreased as it exited the Columbia Gorge, depositing the Portland delta which today is about 200 square miles and 80 m deep. The cities of Portland, Oregon, and Vancouver, Washington, are built on the delta. The flood water then backwashed up the Willamette Valley to Eugene, Oregon, layering the valley with 15 to 25 feet of Palouse silt. As a result of the Missoula Flood, the Willamette Valley is a rich agricultural area with topsoil "stolen" from Washington State.

For many years no one knew about the Lake Missoula Flood. Then J Harlen Bretz (his first name is just the letter "J"), a geologist, discovered evidence of a gigantic flood, the Lake Missoula flood. It was remarkable that he connected the dots from new topographic maps and exploration of eastern Washington that revealed the features could only have been formed by a flood so large that it staggered the imagination. But his ideas were rejected for 40 years. They were ridiculed as an "outrageous hypothesis," because, as some geologists said, it was too biblical in scale. Bretz did not know the source of the water for 10 years, which did not help his case.

Bretz also interpreted the sand/silt layers in the Walla Walla river valley as pulses of increasing and decreasing flow as temporary Lake Lewis was filling. The pulses were actually caused by rising and lowering water levels in the lake sending waves up the tributary valleys. The rising and falling water levels of Lake Lewis were a result of converging and diverging water flows in the path of the Flood in eastern Washington.

With the advent of aerial photography, the hundreds of pieces of evidence for the flood persuaded the geological establishment in the 1960s that indeed there was a gigantic Lake Missoula flood. However, they also determined that a volcanic ash layer near the top of the sand/silt layers in the Walla Walla river valley was from an eruption of Mount St. Helens. In the 1980s, Richard Waitt pointed out that it was very improbable that two very rare events occurred at the same time. Therefore, Waitt claimed that each sand/silt layer represented a different stupendous Lake Missoula flood, separated by around 50 years or so, allowing glacial Lake Missoula to fill again. Since there are 40 sand/silt layers, his idea resulted in the belief of 40 separate huge Lake Missoula floods. Later, geologists hypothesized there were more than 90 floods, which they based on other geological features just north of Grand Coulee Dam.

I have thoroughly investigated the claim of 90 floods and found obvious evidence that there was only one gigantic Lake Missoula flood. A team of eight geologists from the University of Alberta at Edmonton came to the same conclusions and published their results in 1999 in the journal *Geology*. [3]Out of a half dozen pieces of evidence for one gigantic flood is the fact that the sand/silt layers in the Walla Walla River Valley show *no erosion* within and between the layers. Erosion is an expected result from fast flood currents in super floods. Bretz was correct in his original assessment of the origin of each sand/silt layer.

The great Lake Missoula flood is an amazing story of "detective" work, of its rejection despite hundreds of pieces of evidence, of its eventual acceptance, of the great amount of geological work a super flood can cause, and of the mindset of geologists back then—and even today.

1. Oard, M.J., *The Missoula Flood Controversy and the Genesis Flood*. Creation Research Society Books, Glendale, AZ, 2004.

2. Oard, M.J., *The Great Missoula Flood: Modern Day Evidence for the Worldwide Flood*, Awesome Science Media, Amherst, VA, 2014.

3. Shaw, J., Munro-Stasiuk, M., Sawyer, B., Beanery, C., Lesemann, J.-E., Musacchio, A., Rains, B., and Young, R.R., The Channeled Scabland: Back to Bretz? Geology, 27(1999), pp. 605- 608.

HIT or MISS

IF THE MISSOULA FLOOD HAPPENED TODAY, WOULD YOU BE DEAD OR DRY?

Seattle, WA : You survived! Only, this is the Ice Age, so you're sitting under thousands of feet of packed ice and snow...

Tri-Cities, WA: You died under 700 feet of water. Welcome to temporary Lake Lewis!

Spokane, WA: The waters roared over the Spokane Valley at a depth of about 600'. You're *so* dead.

Portland, OR: 400' under. Sorry.

Here's a list of the depth of the floodwaters (in feet) over the Willamette Valley, OR.

Albany – 188'

Aloha -186'

Amity – 400'

Aumsvilla - 37'

Beaverton Mall - 210'

Broadmead - 217'

Brownville - 44'

Buel - 15'

Buena Vista - 140'

Canby - 247'

Cheshire - 71'

Clackamas Town Center - 225'

Coburg - Your feet got wet.

Colton - You survived!

Corvallis - 175'

Cottage Grove - You survived!

Creswell - You survived!

Dallas - 74'

Dawson - 60'

Downtown Portland - 380'

Estacada - You survived!

Eugene (airport) 30'

Eugene - (downtown) You survived! (barely)

Falls City - 30'

Gervais - 216'

Gresham - 77'

Halsey - 120'

Harrisburg   91'

Hillsboro - 250'

Horton - You survived!

Independence – 224'

Janzten Beach – 379'

Jasper – You survived!

Jefferson – 170'

Junction City – 73'

Keizer – 266'

Lake Oswego (City Center) – 240'

Lebanon - 54'

Lewisburg – 159'

Lorane – You survived!

Lowell – You survived!

Maplewood – You survived! (barely)

Marcola – You survived!

Marion – 100'

McMinnville – 240'

Monroe – 112'

Mount Angel – 232'

Mount Scott – You survived!

Mount Tabor – You survived!

Mt. Pisgah – You survived!

Mulino – 163'

Natron – 400'

Newberg – 187'

Noti – You survived!

Oakville – 157'

OHSU Campus – You survived!

Philomath – 120'

Pittock Mansion – You survived!

Portland Intl Airport – 373'

Portland State Univ. – 200'

Powell Butte – You survived!

Rocky Butte – You survived!

Salem (airport) – 190'

Salem (downtown) – 204'

Salem (South Hills) – You survived!

Scotts Mill – Your feet got wet, but you survived!

Sheridan – 250'

Silverton – 150'

Skinner Butte – You survived!

Sodaville – You survived! (barely)

Springfield – You survived!

Thurston - You survived!

Troutdale Airport – 365'

Turner – 115'

Veneta – puddles.

Washburn Butte – 262'

Washington Park Zoo – You survived!

Washington Square – 170'

Willamina – 175'

Yamhill – 210'

LAURENTIDE ICE SHEET
Seattle
Olympia
Spokane
To Lake Missoula
Tri-Cities
Glacial Lake Lewis
Wallula Gap
Portland
ICE AGE COASTLINE
THE PATH
OF THE
MISSOULA FLOOD

JOIN MY NEWSLETTER

Sign up for updates and discounts!

https://shannonskaer.com/newsletter/

SHare THIS STOrY WITH a frienD

- Do you or a friend live in the path of the Missoula Flood?

- Do you know someone crazy enough to be "into" apocalyptic disasters?

- Do you have a friend who needs to know about the Missoula Flood?

Share the link below or text a photo of the QR code to let your friends download a free digital copy of this book and experience the disaster for themselves. (If they choose to download the book they'll also be subscribed to my author newsletter. They can unsubscribe at any time. I won't be offended.)

https://shannonskaer.com/freebook/

ABOUT THE AUTHOR

One of Shannon's favorite books as a kid was *The World's Last Mysteries* by Reader's Digest. It chronicled "ancient civilizations, archaeological discoveries, unexplained catastrophes, and other mysteries from man's past." Or, in other words, exactly the kind of thing she geeks out over.

As an author of historical and science fiction, she enjoys exploring forgotten peoples and vanished places from a Christian worldview informed by creation science. You can find out more about her and her upcoming book, *City of the Gods, A Tale of the Tower of Babel* online at www.shannonskae r.com

ACKNOWLEDGEMENTS

For a short piece of fiction, this story has covered almost as many miles as the flood itself. I would like to thank Lloyd DeKay, Ice Age Floods Insitute Gorge Chapter President, author Michael Oard, Rick and Sylvia Thompson, and Geologist Brittany Martin for their advice and expertise. Thanks to Holly Sullivan for reading all of the drafts, to Adam for helping me with *all* the things, Kassie for making me go deeper, Cara for teaching me what that meant, and to Kevin and Michelle for making this possible. You're the best!